For Maya

Thank you to Romina, Joe, Rhode, Dan B., and Jamie B.

Carolrhoda Books
A division of Lerner Publishing Group, Inc.
241 First Avenue North
Minneapolis, MN 55401 U.S.A.

Website address: www.lernerbooks.com

Library of Congress Cataloging-in-Publication Data

Hiti, Samuel.
    Waga's big scare / written and illustrated by Samuel Hiti.
       p.   cm.
    Summary: Waga the monster's scare is lost, and Waga must find it by morning or risk disappearing
forever.
    ISBN 978–0–7613–5622–6 (lib. bdg. : alk. paper)
    [1. Monsters—Fiction. 2. Lost and found possessions—Fiction. 3. Fear—Fiction.] I. Title.
PZ7.H62966Wag 2012
[E]—dc23   2012000315

Manufactured in the United States of America
1 – DP – 7/15/12

WAGA'S BIG SCARE

By SAMUEL HITI

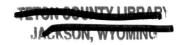 CAROLRHODA BOOKS MINNEAPOLIS

WAGA IS A MONSTER.

Waga isn't as big, tall, hairy, slimy, scaly, oozy, lumpy, or bumpy as the other monsters.

But don't let that fool you.

And Waga is not afraid to use it.

Oh no, look at Waga.

Waga is Sad.

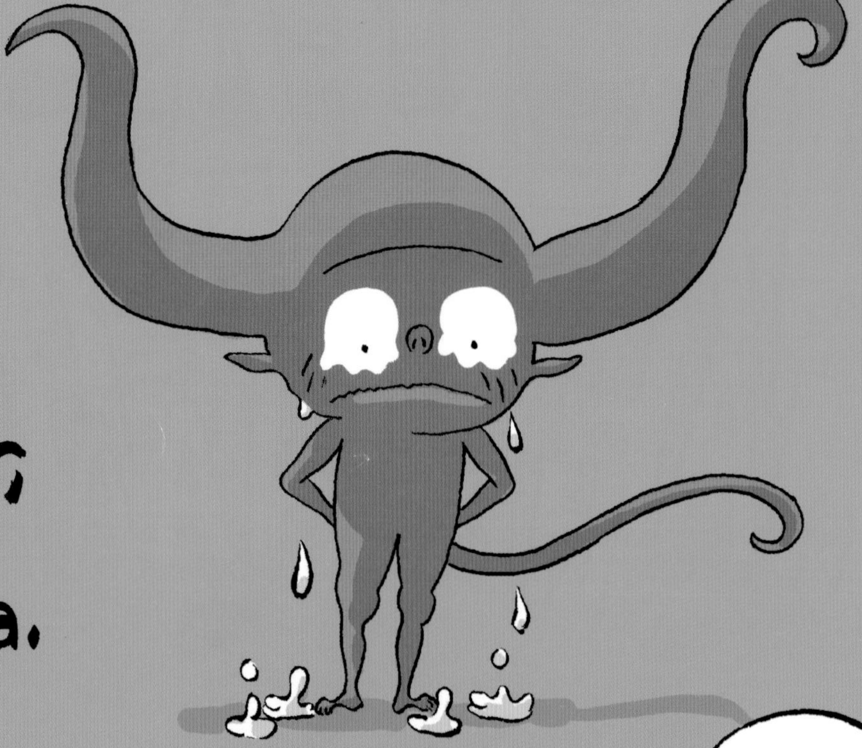

Poor, Sad Waga.

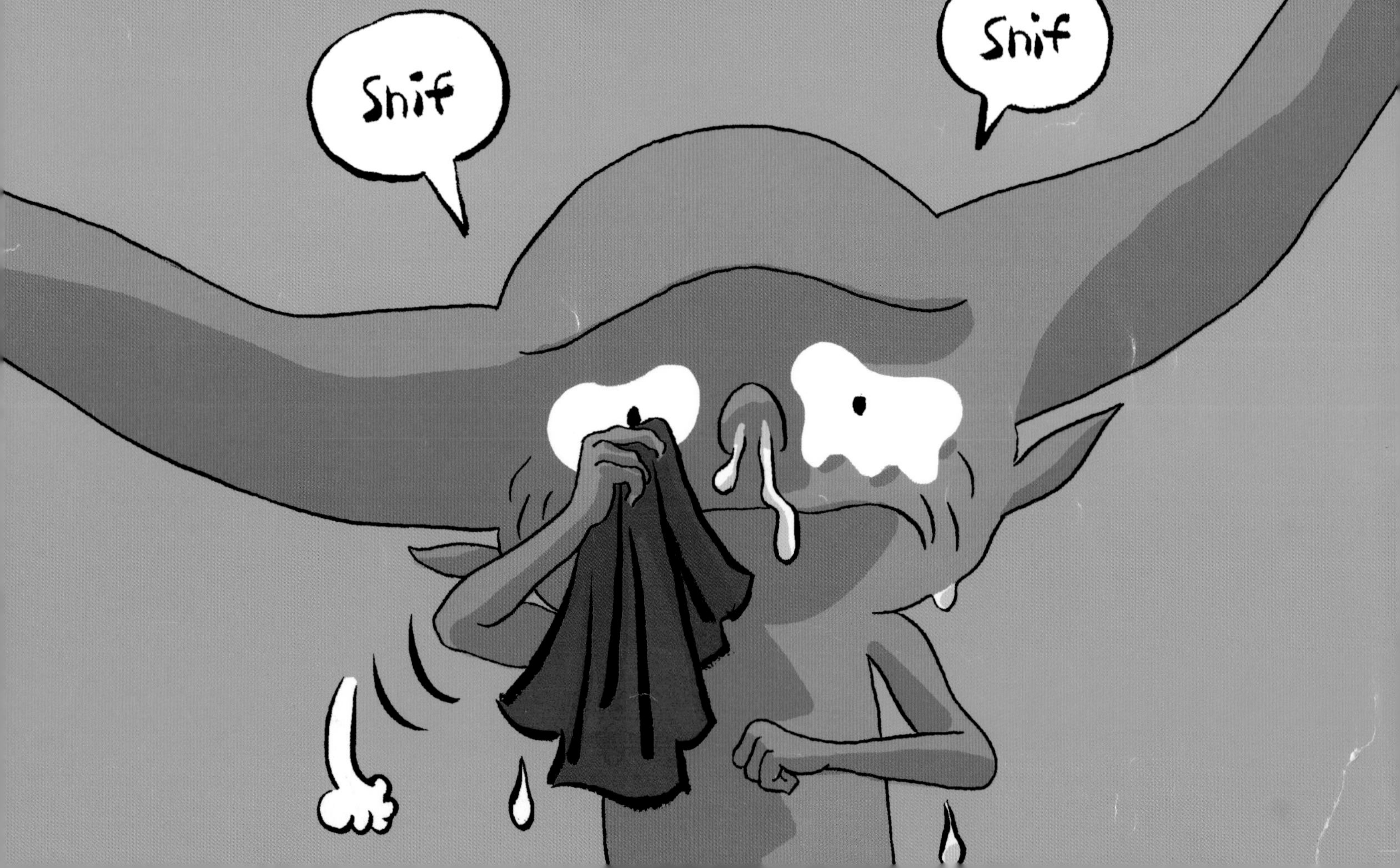

Waga needs to find THE SCARE
before morning comes.

Otherwise, Waga will disappear for good.

Waga had better do something quick.

Waga's SCARE has to be around somewhere,

BUT WHERE?

Waga thinks and thinks.

Waga starts looking for clues.

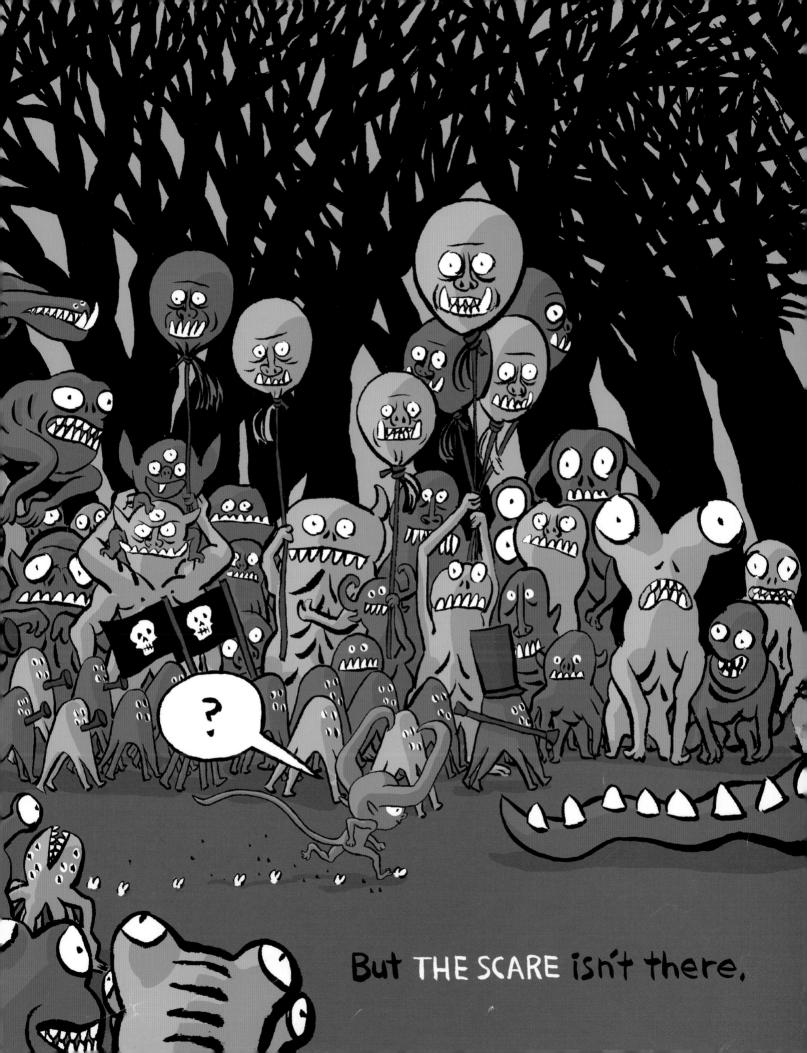

But THE SCARE isn't there,

Waga rushes through the graveyard.

Waga scours every
nook and cranny.

The sun is almost up.

Poor, poor Waga.

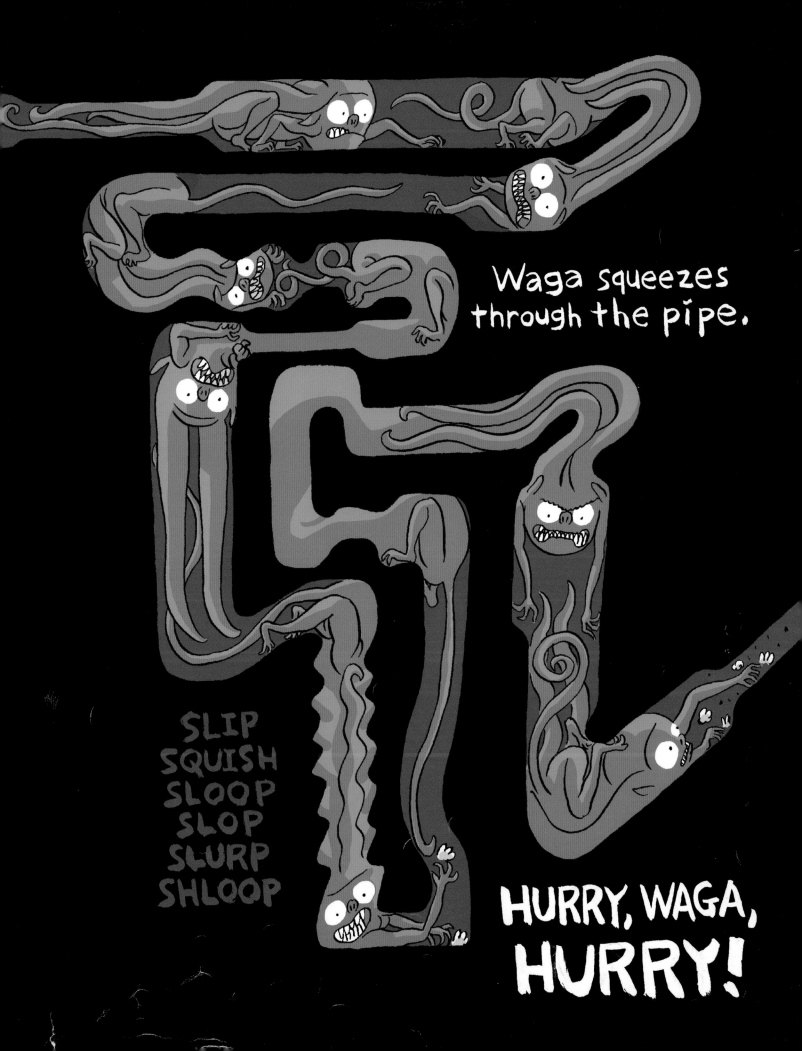

Waga squeezes through the pipe.

SLIP
SQUISH
SLOOP
SLOP
SLURP
SHLOOP

HURRY, WAGA,
HURRY!

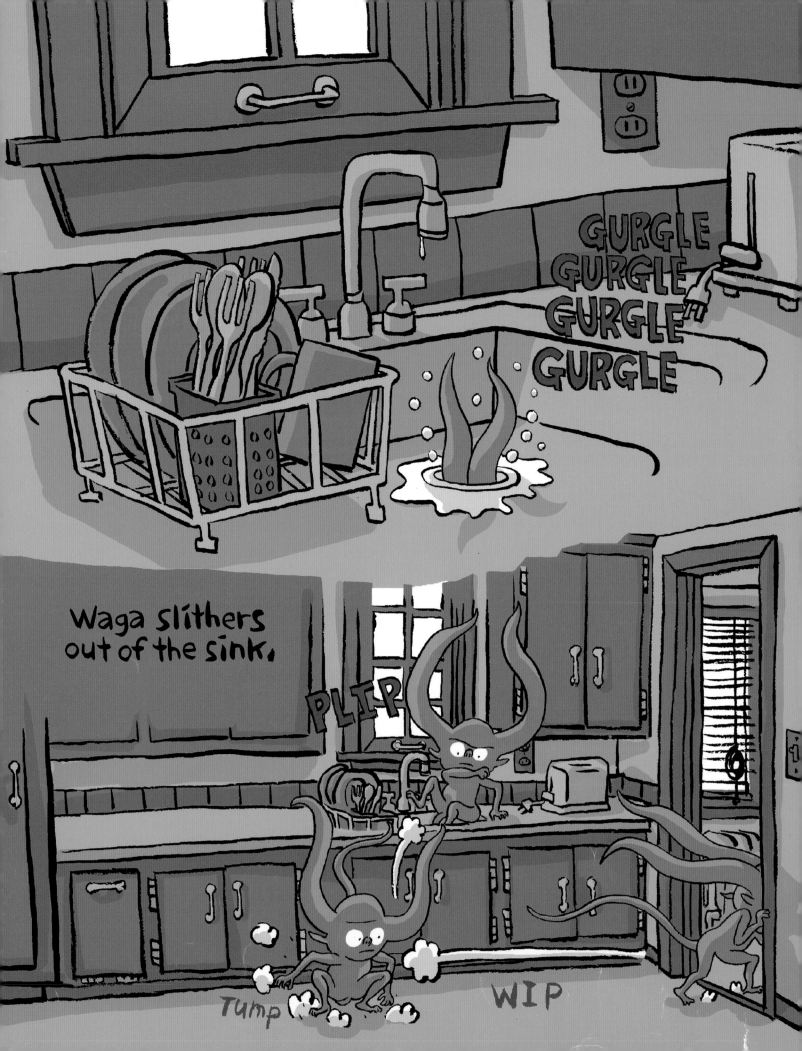

JUMBO

THE BOY

AND

ARNOLD

THE ELEPHANT

Dan Greenburg

JUMBO

THE BOY
—— AND ——
ARNOLD

THE ELEPHANT

ILLUSTRATED BY

Susan Perl

HARPER & ROW, PUBLISHERS

Jumbo the Boy and Arnold the Elephant
Text copyright © 1969 by Dan Greenburg
Illustrations copyright © 1969 by Susan Perl,
© 1989 by Harper & Row, Publishers, Inc.

Printed in Singapore. All rights reserved.
1   2   3   4   5   6   7   8   9   10

Library of Congress Cataloging-in-Publication Data
Greenburg, Dan.
    Jumbo the boy and Arnold the elephant / by Dan Greenburg : illustrated by Susan Perl.
        p.   cm.
    Summary: Problems arise in two households when a mix-up at the
hospital sends a baby elephant home with human parents and a baby
boy to the zoo.
    ISBN 0-06-022277-8 : $
    ISBN 0-06-022278-6 (lib. bdg.) : $
    [1. Elephants—Fiction.]   I. Perl, Susan, 1922-   ill.   II. Title.
PZ7.G8278Ju 1989   87-24931
[E]—dc19   CIP
                                                          AC

For Zack the Boy

Once upon a time a very peculiar thing happened. Two babies were born on the same day at a large hospital in the middle of town. Not so peculiar, you say? Just let me continue.

Due to a very silly mix-up, each of these babies was accidentally given to the other one's mother instead of to his own. You still won't appreciate just how silly this mix-up really was until I tell you that one of the babies was a little boy, and the other baby was a little elephant.

Now I can't tell you exactly how such a silly mix-up happened, but I do know that the nurse who got the babies mixed up was, in the first place, very nearsighted. And, in the second place, this nurse was a silly person who was never able to admit it when she made a mistake.

Anyway, when the nurse brought the little elephant in to the mother of the little boy, the mother of the little boy was puzzled.

"He is a very lovely baby," she said, because she didn't want to hurt the baby's feelings, "but are you sure this is really *my* baby? I mean, are you sure there hasn't been any mistake?"

"There hasn't been any mistake, madam," said the silly nurse. "I never make mistakes."

"I see," said the mother of the little boy. "Well, if you're sure there hasn't been any mistake, I suppose you know best. Let's have him."

The silly nurse gave the little elephant to the little boy's mother, and although the little boy's mother still wasn't entirely convinced that there hadn't been a mistake, she was too polite to argue.

After all, the little elephant may not have looked exactly as she had expected her baby to look, but then, he *was* a very cute little baby. And, as she later told her husband, "Babies sometimes look a little peculiar when they're born. I'm sure that he'll begin to look more like a little boy as he begins to grow."

When the nurse brought the little boy baby in to the mother of the little elephant, the mother of the little elephant was puzzled too.

"He is a very lovely baby," she said, because she, too, didn't want to hurt the baby's feelings, "but are you sure this is really *my* baby? I mean, are you sure there hasn't been any mistake?"

"There hasn't been any mistake, madam," said the silly nurse. "I never make mistakes."

"I see," said the mother of the little elephant. "Well, if you're sure there hasn't been any mistake, I suppose you know best. Let's have him."

The silly nurse gave the little boy to the little elephant's mother, and although the little elephant's mother still wasn't entirely convinced that there hadn't been a mistake, she was just as polite as the little boy's mother and didn't want to argue.

After all, the little boy may not have looked exactly as she had expected her baby to look, but then, he *was* a very cute little baby. And, as she later told her husband, "Babies sometimes look a little peculiar when they're born. I'm sure that he'll begin to look more like a little elephant as he begins to grow."

In a few days both mothers were allowed to take their babies home. The mother of the little boy took her little elephant back to a cozy house uptown, and the mother of the little elephant took her little boy back to a cozy cage in the zoo downtown.

Friends of both families came to see the babies, and if they were a bit surprised by what they saw, they were too polite to say anything that would hurt the parents' feelings.

"Say, that's some baby you've got there," they said. "Just look at that baby," they said. "He certainly is...unusual, isn't he?"

The people who had the little elephant decided to call him Arnold. They brought him lots of toys and they fed him very nicely and they played with him a great deal, and they tried very hard to pretend that he was just a normal little boy.

"Arnold is making rapid progress," they kept telling one another. "Arnold seems to be doing very nicely." Quietly they would add: "Of course, his ears and his nose appear to be making a lot more rapid progress than the *rest* of him, and, well, there *is* the tail...."

But then they would try to look on the bright side, and they would say: "Baby frogs have tails when they're tadpoles that drop off when they grow up, so maybe when Arnold grows up, his tail will drop off too."

As it happens, Arnold was a very smart little elephant, and a very cuddly one too, so before long the people who had him began to love him very much and hardly noticed the ears, the nose, and the tail.

Sometimes, when they were in a particularly good mood, they even thought they could see in Arnold some faint family resemblance, although it's true the father felt that Arnold resembled the *mother*'s side of the family, and the mother felt that Arnold resembled the *father*'s.

Arnold was, for the most part, very happy. He loved the people who took care of him and he knew they loved him too. But he also knew that he was different from other little boys, and he sometimes felt he was funny-looking, and now and then, when nobody was looking, he occasionally permitted himself to cry.

The elephants who had the little boy decided to call him Jumbo. They brought him lots of peanuts and they fed him very nicely and they played with him a great deal, and they tried very hard to pretend that he was just a normal little elephant.

"Jumbo is making rapid progress," they kept telling one another. "Jumbo seems to be doing very nicely."

Quietly they would add: "Of course, his ears and his trunk don't seem to be developing very rapidly, and I'm not sure I can see the tail yet at all...."

But then they would try to look on the bright side and they would say: "Baby deer don't have antlers when they're fawns and only develop them when they grow up, so maybe when Jumbo grows up he'll develop a trunk, a tail, and bigger ears too."

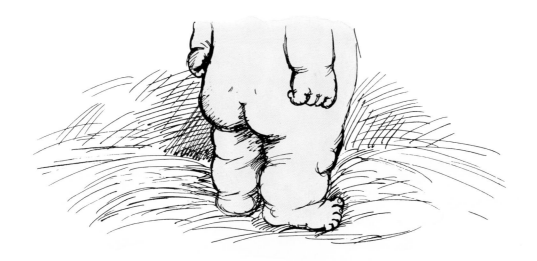

Jumbo, like Arnold, was also very smart and very cuddly, and so before long the elephants who had him began to love him very much and hardly noticed the lack of ears, trunk, and tail.

Even when they were in a particularly good mood, however, the elephants never noticed any family resemblance in Jumbo. This was partly because Jumbo looked nothing at all like an elephant, and partly because elephants don't care about things like family resemblances.

Jumbo, for the most part, was very happy. He loved the elephants who took care of him and he knew they loved him too. But he also knew he was different from other little elephants, and he sometimes felt he was funny-looking, and now and then, when nobody was looking, he occasionally permitted himself to cry.

As time passed, I am sorry to report, Jumbo became more and more upset about his looks. His parents were careful not to hurt Jumbo's feelings, and whenever ears or trunks or tails were mentioned in his presence they were always quick to add some reassuring comment such as: "Tails are such a nuisance, Jumbo—you ought to be glad you don't have one."

But although Jumbo knew they only said these things to make him feel better, it made him cry every time.

One day, what Jumbo's parents prayed would never happen did happen. Some little elephants from a cage all the way over on the other side of the elephant house saw Jumbo and began to call him names.

"Hey, Tiny Ears!" they called. "Hey, Trunkless!" "Hey, Mr. No-Tail!"

Jumbo ran into the darkest corner of his cage and hid under a huge pile of straw.

When his parents heard what had happened, they were furious. They told the parents of the bad little elephants what had happened and recommended that they be severely punished.

But no matter how they pleaded with poor Jumbo, he still would not come out from under the pile of straw.

"I am ugly," he said. "I don't look like other elephants. I don't want anyone to look at me anymore."

Mother and Father Elephant were quite upset.

"We must help poor Jumbo feel he is just like all the other elephants," they said, "but how?"

Then Father Elephant had a plan. He went and got some cardboard and some glue and some rope and a pair of scissors, and he went busily to work. When he was done, he seemed quite pleased.

"Look at these, Mother," he said to his wife. "Now Jumbo will look like all the other elephants." And he showed her what he had made: two large gray cardboard ears, a long gray cardboard trunk, and a little tufted rope of a tail.

When Jumbo saw what Father Elephant had made, he seemed a little happier.

"Do you really think they will work?" he said.

"Try them on," said Father Elephant.

And Jumbo did.

"They feel pretty funny," said Jumbo. "How do they look?"

"Terrific," said Father Elephant. "A hundred haystacks high." (The highest praise an elephant can give anyone is to tell him he looks a hundred haystacks high.)

"That good, eh?" said Jumbo.

"A hundred haystacks—maybe even a hundred and ten," said Mother Elephant, exaggerating in her excitement.

Jumbo appeared satisfied and went off to play, feeling for the first time that he looked like other elephants. But as soon as he was gone, Mother and Father Elephant shook their heads and looked at each other sadly.

"I'm afraid we told a fib," said Father Elephant.

"He still doesn't look much like an elephant," said Mother Elephant.

"He looks about as much like an elephant as I look like a kangaroo," said Father Elephant.

"You know," said Mother Elephant, "while it's true Jumbo doesn't look like an elephant, he *does* look like *some* animal or other. I wish I could think of which one it could be."

"Yes," Father Elephant agreed. "Perhaps if we could think of what animal Jumbo looks like, we might be able to help him better."

They both sat down and tried to picture what kind of animal it was that Jumbo looked like.

"Jumbo's ears and nose are small, and so are those of a giraffe," said Mother Elephant. "Maybe he's a giraffe."

They tried to picture Jumbo as a giraffe.

"No," said Father Elephant. "His neck isn't long enough, and besides he doesn't have a tail. Jumbo's no giraffe. But maybe he's...a giant panda."

"Yes," said Mother Elephant excitedly. "A giant panda hardly has any tail at all, and it has small ears like Jumbo and no trunk. Maybe he *is* a giant panda."

"No," said Father Elephant, "the markings are all wrong, and Jumbo hardly has any fur at all, except for that tiny

patch of it on his head. I'm afraid he's no giant panda either. But maybe he's...an orangutan."

"Yes!" said Mother Elephant. "An orangutan has much less fur than a giant panda, and there's a little patch of it on top of its head like Jumbo has, and I forget whether an orangutan has a tail or not, but if it does it can't be very big. Maybe Jumbo *is* an orangutan."

They tried to picture Jumbo as an orangutan.

"Nope," said Father Elephant at last, "an orangutan is close, but that's not quite it either. Jumbo's arms aren't quite that long, and his face is sort of different, and he doesn't have even as much fur as an orangutan. No, unless I'm really badly mistaken, I don't think that an orangutan is what Jumbo is either. I think we're pretty close, though. I think we're really pretty close. Now then, what looks like an orangutan but isn't?"

"What looks like an orangutan but isn't?" said Mother Elephant. "Hmmm, let me think. I know—a gorilla!"

They tried to picture Jumbo as a gorilla, but that didn't work out either.

"A chimpanzee?" said Father Elephant.

But that wasn't it either.

"A duck-billed platypus!" said Mother Elephant.

"*A duck-billed platypus?*" said Father Elephant. "Is that what you said—a duck-billed platypus?"

"Uh, yeah, Why?" said Mother Elephant.

"Do you know what a duck-billed platypus *looks* like?" said Father Elephant.

"Well, I guess not," said Mother Elephant.

"Hmmmph!" said Father Elephant. "A duck-billed platypus indeed. Jumbo looks as much like a duck-billed platypus as he does a…a…as he looks like Mr. Stiles, our zookeeper."

Father Elephant's eyes suddenly grew very wide.

"Wait—*that's it!*" he said. Father Elephant began to jump up and down with excitement. "That's it, that's it!" he cried.

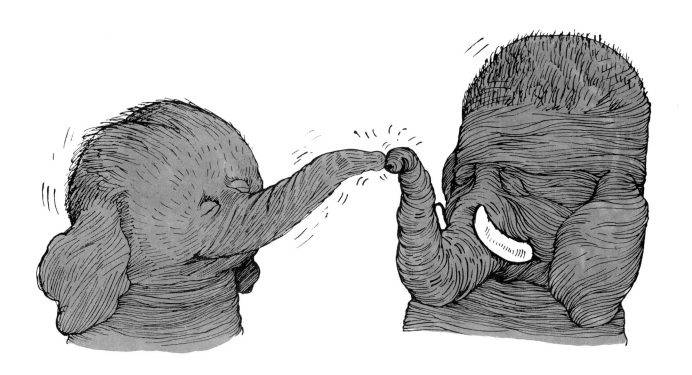

"Jumbo is a baby zookeeper?" said Mother Elephant.

"No, a baby *human being*—that's what Jumbo is, a baby *human being*!"

"Father, you're a genius," said Mother Elephant, and kissed him on the tip of the trunk. "You're absolutely right. Now that I think of it, Jumbo looks exactly like the human beings who come to see us here on the other side of the bars. But how do you suppose I could have given birth to a baby human being instead of to a baby elephant?"

"That is something I do not know," said Father Elephant. "After all, I am only an elephant. Perhaps we should ask somebody who is really smart, like Mr. Stiles."

And so Father and Mother Elephant waited until Mr. Stiles came by to feed them that evening, and then they whispered their suspicions in his ear.

"Hmmmm," said Mr. Stiles, "a baby human being, eh? Very interesting, very interesting. I *had* noticed he looked kind of strange for a baby elephant, but I didn't say anything about it, not wanting to offend you folks. But since you've brought the matter up yourselves, let me take a close look at the little tyke and then do a bit of thinking."

Mr. Stiles walked over to Jumbo and took a long hard look at him.

"I don't know," said Mr. Stiles. "I didn't think so before, but he sure looks like an elephant to me *now*. Baby human beings don't have big ears and trunks and tails like that, you know."

"Oh, those are just cardboard," said Father Elephant. "We made them for him so he'd look more like an elephant, that's all. Take off your ears and trunk and tail a moment, Jumbo. Let Mr. Stiles get a good look at you."

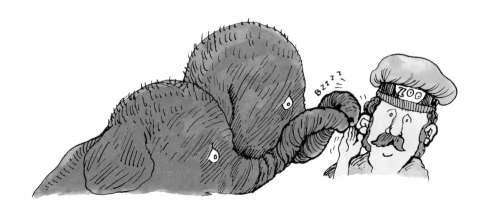

Embarrassed, Jumbo took off his ears and trunk and tail. Mr. Stiles took a close look at him, then cocked his head and whistled.

"Boy," said Mr. Stiles, "you folks are sure right. I've got to hand it to you. That's a baby human being if I've ever seen one."

"The thing we can't figure out," said Mother Elephant, "is how I could have given birth to a baby human being instead of to an elephant."

"Maybe you didn't," said Mr. Stiles.

"Whatever do you mean?" said Mother Elephant.

"I'll explain later," said Mr. Stiles. "First, I'm going to do a little investigating of my own. See you folks in the morning."

And then he was gone.

Mr. Stiles looked up the date of Jumbo's birth in the records of the zoo office. Then he looked up the hospital that Jumbo was born in. Then he made a lot of phone calls. Then he went to bed.

The following morning, a large truck pulled up outside the cozy uptown house of Jumbo's real mother and father. Mr. Stiles got out of the truck, walked up to the door of the house, and rang the bell.

Presently the door opened and a tiny elephant dressed in short pants, a polo shirt, and sneakers said: "Who is it, please?"

"I'm Mr. Stiles from the zoo," said Mr. Stiles. "And who are you?"

"I'm Arnold," said Arnold.

"Hello, Arnold," said Mr. Stiles.

Just then a woman came to the door.

"Yes?" she said. "Can I help you?"

"My name is Stiles, ma'am," said Mr. Stiles. "I'm from the zoo. I wonder if I could show you something."

"Well, I suppose so," she said. "What is it you want to show me?"

"Just a minute," said Mr. Stiles. He walked back to the truck. He opened the back doors of the truck and motioned someone inside to come out.

After a moment a big elephant lumbered out of the truck, followed by a middle-sized elephant, followed by a very tiny something or other that looked a little like an elephant but wasn't. They all followed Mr. Stiles shyly up the walk.

"Why, what is this?" said the woman. "I don't understand."

Just then the woman's husband came to the door and saw the elephants. "What's going on out here?" he said.

And then it happened.

Almost at the same instant, the woman somehow realized who Jumbo was, and Mother Elephant somehow realized who Arnold was, and the next thing anybody knew both the man and the woman had scooped up Jumbo in their arms and Mother and Father Elephant had scooped up Arnold in their trunks, and everybody was laughing and crying at the same time.

"Are you my real mom and dad?" said Jumbo.

"Yes, precious," said Jumbo's real mom and dad.

"Then I guess I'm not a funny-looking elephant after all, am I?" said Jumbo.

"No," said Jumbo's real mom and dad, "you're a handsome little boy."

"And I guess I'm not a funny-looking little boy after all," said Arnold.

"No," said Mother and Father Elephant, "you're a handsome little elephant."

"Well," said Mr. Stiles, "I guess I'd be safe in assuming that you folks wouldn't mind if I left Jumbo here with you and took Arnold back to the zoo with his real parents. Right?"

Everybody was just about to agree when suddenly they realized what was really happening.

"You know, Mr. Stiles," said Jumbo's real mom and dad, "we've gotten to love Arnold just like he was our own son."

"Yes," said Arnold, "how can I leave these wonderful people, Mr. Stiles?"

"And we've gotten to love Jumbo just like he was *our* own son," said Mother and Father Elephant.

"How can I leave these wonderful elephants, Mr. Stiles?" said Jumbo.

Mr. Stiles sighed.

"Well, you can't all move into this house here," he said, "and I certainly can't have you all moving into the elephant house at the zoo...."

Everyone looked expectantly at Mr. Stiles.

"I'll tell you what," said Mr. Stiles. "I'll leave Jumbo here with you and take Arnold back to the zoo like I said before. But every Saturday morning I'll come by bright and early and take all three of you people to the zoo for the day so you can all visit with each other. Now, how's that?"

"Mr. Stiles," said Jumbo's real mom and dad, "you are a genius."

"Mr. Stiles," said Mother and Father Elephant, "you are a hundred haystacks high."

"A hundred haystacks high?" said Arnold the elephant. "What does *that* mean?"

"Oh, that's elephant talk, Arnold," said Jumbo the boy. "I'll teach you all about it next Saturday."

And so all the elephants went back to their cozy cage in the zoo downtown, and all the people went into their cozy house uptown, and everybody lived happily ever after.